English text copyright © 2013 by NorthSouth Books Inc., New York 10016.
First published in Belgium under the title *Boum Boum Boum Qui est là?*
Copyright © 2012 by Mijade Publications (B-5000 Namur – Belgium)
Text & illustrations © 2012 by Philippe Goossens
Designed by Pamela Darcy.

First published in the United States, Great Britain, Canada, Australia, and New Zealand in
2013 by NorthSouth Books Inc., an imprint of NordSüd Verlag AG, CH-8005 Zürich, Switzerland.
Distributed in the United States by NorthSouth Books Inc., New York 10016.

Library of Congress Cataloging-in-Publication Data is available.
Printed in Belgium by Proost N.V., B-2300 Turnhout, August 2012.

ISBN: 978-0-7358-4122-2
1 3 5 7 9 · 10 8 6 4 2
www.northsouth.com

Knock! Knock! Knock! Who's There?

PHILIPPE GOOSSENS

North
South

KNOCK! KNOCK!

What? Who's there . . . ?

Boo! Booooooo! Boo!

It's cold outside.
Let me in!

BooOOooohoooooOOOO!

What a strange voice.
It sounds like . . .

a ghooooooost!

KNOCK! KNOCK! KNOCK!

KNOCK!

Who's there?

Let me in.
I'm hungry!

He's hungry?
Then it must be . . .

an ogre!

KNOCK! KNOCK! KNOCK!

Who's there?

**Hurry up!
I'm ravenous!**

Help me! This is decidedly . . .

The BiG
BaD
Wolf!

KNOCK! KNOCK! KNOCK!

Who's there?

**Now . . . let me in,
or I will turn you into a slimy slug!**

I'm sure it's . . .

a wicked witch!

KNOCK! KNOCK! KNOCK!

Go away!
I do not open the door to strangers.

But I'm not a stranger!

It's me, Archibald!

It's you!
You scared me!

Yes, and I've got a surprise for you. . . . .